THE
LORD
OF
FIRE

by

JAMES LOVEGROVE

The 5 Lords of Pain
Book 5

First published in 2010 in Great Britain by
Barrington Stoke Ltd
18 Walker Street, Edinburgh, EH3 7LP

www.barringtonstoke.co.uk

ISBN: 978-1-84299-817-5

Printed in Great Britain by Bell & Bain Ltd

Check out the 5 Lords of Pain
website:

www.fivelordsofpain.co.uk

For amazing downloads,
competitions and
behind-the-scenes action!

The 5 Lords of Pain Books

Contents

The Story So Far

The Contest takes place every 30 years. It's a series of duels between five demons and a single human champion. What's at stake is nothing less than the fate of the world.

The human champion is always a member of the Yamada family. The task of defeating the demons, who are known as the Five Lords of Pain, is passed down from father to son. It has been that way for many hundreds of years.

Tom Yamada is the latest in line to face the Five Lords. Tom is only fifteen, and his Contest isn't due to start until he is 30. Something has gone wrong, however. Now Tom finds himself having to fight the duels long before he is supposed to.

Tom has won the first four duels, beating the Lord of the Mountain, the Lord of the Void, the Lord of Tears, and the Lord of the Typhoon.

But it turns out that Tom's *sensei*, Dragon, is not all he seems to be. Dragon is in fact the fifth Lord of Pain, the Lord of Fire. All along, he has been pretending to be a human in order to get close to Tom and steal from him the objects which gave the other four Lords of Pain their powers, their Element Gems.

Now that Dragon has the Element Gems, it seems he can't be stopped. However, he has agreed to face Tom in one final duel. It's a fight Tom knows he has very little chance of winning.

Chapter 1

Scars

Tom brushed his teeth, scowling into the bathroom mirror.

The face that scowled back at him was not the face he'd been used to seeing. Not any more.

One side of it was horribly scarred. The scars crossed Tom's cheek in three jagged lines which ran from his ear to the corner of his mouth, thick and red and ugly. They twisted up the whole of that side of his face. The sight of them made Tom feel sick inside. He wanted to close his eyes and pretend the scars weren't there.

But he forced himself to keep on looking at them.

The more he looked, the angrier he got. And the angrier he got, the less he was afraid.

Tom had a lot to be afraid of.

There was less than a week to go till his duel with the Lord of Fire.

Less than a week to go till the end of the world.

Tom told himself not to think that way. He could still defeat the Lord of Fire. He could still win the Contest.

Yeah, right.

The Lord of Fire had the Element Gems of the other four Lords of Pain. He had all their powers, as well as his own.

Also, the Lord of Fire was Dragon. Dragon had been Tom's *sensei* for seven years. There was nothing Tom knew about combat that Dragon didn't know, and there was plenty Dragon knew that Tom didn't.

In other words, Tom was about to face an enemy who had every chance of winning. It was like a mouse getting ready to fight a lion. The Lord of Fire could crush Tom easily, and then the world would be his for the taking. He would lead an army of demons across the earth, burning and killing wherever they went.

Tom scrubbed his teeth really hard, as if he was trying to wear them down to stubs. At last he stopped and spat toothpaste foam into the basin. There were streaks of blood in the foam.

He stopped brushing because his hand had begun to hurt. Till the week before, Tom had been wearing a plaster cast on his wrist and hand to allow the bones of his broken finger to set. The finger had healed now, but the joint still hurt if Tom used the hand for too long.

Tom's chest hurt sometimes too. The Lord of the Typhoon had broken one of his ribs during their duel. The Lord of the Typhoon had also given Tom the scars on his face.

The broken ribs and scarred face were bad. But it was the pain from the broken finger that Tom minded the most. It was a sharp throbbing that reminded him that he had been betrayed by someone he'd trusted.

Dragon had broken the finger.

Dragon had tricked Tom.

Dragon, who was really the Lord of Fire, had treated Tom as if he were a fool.

He'd used Tom to get to the Element Gems. He'd pretended to be Tom's friend for seven years. He'd helped him beat the other four Lords of Pain.

But all along he'd been plotting against Tom. And Tom had had no idea who he really was. He'd been completely taken in by Dragon.

The man Tom had trusted most was now his worst enemy.

Tom glared at himself in the mirror.

His image, with its half-twisted face, glared back at him.

"I'll get you, Lord of Fire," Tom growled. "I'll sort you all right. Just wait and see."

He almost believed what he was saying, too.

Almost.

Chapter 2
What's Important

Tom's mother was in the living room, talking on the phone.

As Tom came out of the bathroom he heard her say, "Thank you, Dr Franks. That's great. I'll let him know you rang. 'Bye."

She put the phone down and turned to Tom.

"That was Dr Franks," she said.

Tom looked blank.

"The consultant from the hospital? The one I told you about the other day?"

"Oh, yeah. Him."

"He just called to say he can see you later this week, if you like. To discuss your ..." Tom's mother pointed at her own cheek, as if the scars were hers, not his. "You know. This."

"My horrible scars, you mean?" said Tom. "My ugly, messed-up face?"

"Don't say that," said his mother. "Dr Franks is sure he can fix your face. He's doing that sort of thing all the time. He's the top plastic surgeon in the country. He ought to be, seeing how much he charges. But that's not the point. I want the best for my boy, and I don't care what it costs."

"That's lovely, Mum. Thanks. I really mean it. Only ..." Tom waited a moment. "I don't want my face to be fixed."

"Oh, come on. You can't be happy with the way you look."

"Of course not. How could I be? I look like ruddy Two-Face from *Batman*. Only an idiot would be happy about that."

"Then what's the problem?" said Tom's mother. "Let's go and see Dr Franks and find out what he can do for you."

"No, not yet."

"Then when?"

"When I'm ready. When this whole thing about the Contest is settled, one way or the other. Until then, I want to keep these scars. I need them. They keep things in focus for me. They remind me what's what."

His mother frowned. "OK, I get it. Or at least I think I get it. But still, you need to do *something*, Tom. Something other than sit around in the flat, which is what you've been doing ever since we got back from Greece. You don't go out any more. You don't see anyone. Sharif's phoned. So has that Debbie Williams girl. They use the landline because your mobile is always switched off, and every time, I've had to lie to them and say you're not in or you're asleep or something. Debbie sounds very nice, by the way. I'd like to meet her some time. Is she your girlfriend?"

"No."

"But you'd like her to be."

"No. Well, yes. Maybe."

"Then, if you want my advice, you'd better stop playing hard to get. That game gets old very quickly."

"I'm not playing hard to get. I just don't want to see Debbie right now, or her to see me."

"Well, OK," said his mother. "What I'm getting at, Tom, is that this isn't doing you any good, the way you're behaving. This isn't right. You can't just hide away from the world and refuse to see anyone."

11

Tom blinked at his mother, and shook his head.

"Have you gone nuts?" he said. "Have you quite forgotten what's going on at the moment? I've got a duel coming up in less than a week. My final duel. Against Dragon, who has the powers of all the Lords of Pain rolled into one. Does that mean nothing to you?"

"Of course it means something to me."

"Then why are you going on about all this stuff, like Sharif and plastic surgeons and Debbie?" Tom said. "None of it matters right now. None of it. The only thing that matters is that I have to win the Contest. If I don't, that's it for the human race. We're finished. The demons take over. End of story."

"I'm well aware of that," replied his mother. "But other things are important too, Tom, even things you say don't matter. Even totally trivial things. You can't just turn your back on normal life."

"Why not? After all, normal life turned its back on me a long time ago. The day I was born, in fact. As soon as I came into the world, I was the next champion for the Contest, and any hope of a normal life for me was gone."

"That may be the case," his mother said. "But I've done my best to raise you in as normal a way as possible, haven't I? If I'd stayed in Japan, you'd have been brought up not just by me but by the whole of the Yamada family. They'd have kept a close watch on you every minute of every day. You'd never have had any freedom. You'd never have had a moment to yourself, to be yourself. Your Great-aunt Akiko would have been breathing down your neck from dawn till dusk. Just think what that would have been like."

Tom did think about it, and shuddered.

"They'd have turned you into a martial arts robot," his mother went on. "You would have had amazing skills in combat, but very few of the other skills you need in life. A bit like your cousin Mai, from the way you describe her."

"She's not so bad really. She's quite fun when you get to know her."

"Even so. I took you away from all that, just because I didn't want you spending the first 30 years of your life as Contest champion and nothing else. I wanted you to be a person as well. Your father, bless him, was a good man, but there were times when he took far too grim a view of life. I loved him in spite of that, and maybe because of it. But it didn't make him easy to get close to. He could be so cold, so distant, bound up in his own sense of duty. I've done my best to make sure you didn't end up the same way, Tom."

"Your point being?"

"My point being, you should go out into the world and meet people, now more than ever," his mother said. "I know you've been staying in because you've been busy keeping up your fitness levels, doing your *kata*, and all of that. You want to have some chance of winning the final duel. You truly want to stop Dragon. And that's great. But you need something else to help you win your fight."

"Oh, yeah? And what's that?"

"Go out and see. Trust me."

Chapter 3
On the Heath

Tom's mother went on for some time, trying to get him to do something normal for a change. In the end Tom gave in, just to shut her up as much as anything. He called Sharif. They arranged to meet on Hampstead Heath for a kick-about. The heath was close to Sharif's house. After the time when he had been attacked and stabbed, Sharif didn't like to stray too far from home. It bothered him not to be near his family.

On the way there, Tom passed a number of people in the street who stared at his face.

They just couldn't help themselves. Their eyes were drawn to his scars like metal to a magnet. Some of them shook their heads and smiled in a friendly way. Others just stared at Tom, as if he was some kind of weird, living work of art.

The day was warm but there was a slight chill in the air, a hint of winter. October had come, bringing cloudy skies with it and turning the trees gold and brown. Halloween was the theme in all the shops. In every window the two main colours were night black and pumpkin orange.

Most years this was Tom's favourite season. He liked Christmas too, but that was really a time for families. Tom didn't have much of a family, just him and his mother. Halloween was better. Halloween was different, it was a time when things got wild and spooky, when kids dressed up in fancy dress and went a bit crazy. Halloween made Tom feel at home. It made him feel less of an oddball and an outsider. All his life, he'd known for a fact that such things as demons did exist. While Halloween lasted, he could believe that the rest of the world knew it too.

Sharif was waiting for him on the edge of Hampstead Heath. It turned out that neither of them had a football with him.

"I thought you were bringing yours," Sharif said.

"I thought you were bringing *yours*," Tom replied.

Sharif smacked his forehead. "D'oh! Right pair of idiots we are. No kick-about, then. What shall we do?"

"I dunno," said Tom. "Just hang out, I suppose."

They walked round the Heath. They watched kids climbing and shouting in the play area. They stood by the pond, where men who thought they were in the Navy were playing

with model speedboats and yachts. They spent
ten minutes on the sidelines at the basketball
court, hoping to be asked to join in the game.
Then they went to the café for a coffee.

"I'm really pee'd off with you, you know,"
Sharif said.

"Why?" Tom hoped Sharif wasn't going to
have a go at him. He knew he hadn't been
much of a friend to Sharif lately, but today, so
far, they'd been getting along fine. It was just
like old times.

"'Cause your scars are so much cooler than
mine," Sharif said.

"You think?"

"Yeah. No one can see any of mine.
They're all on my body, below the neck, hidden
by my clothes. Yours are right out there, you
know what I mean? They're in-your-face."

"They sure are," Tom said.

"Me, I just got stabbed by some sick saddo with a knife," Sharif said. "Happens all the time. You, on the other hand, got attacked by a wild dog in Greece. It tried to bite your face off. That's just mad."

"A wild dog, yeah," said Tom. That was the story he and his mother were telling people. Sharif's brain would have exploded if he'd known the truth – that Tom had been injured by a demon. "It's mad all right."

"Barking mad!" said Sharif, and he started hooting with laughter.

Tom laughed too, although mainly what he found funny was how amused Sharif was by his own joke.

"Listen," Tom said, once Sharif had calmed down. "I just want to say something."

"Uh-oh. Sounds serious."

"I just want to say, you've always been there for me, Sharif. You've always stuck by me, most of all during these past few months when it's been a bit ... difficult. I'm glad to have you as a mate."

"Hey, you've stuck by me too, Tom. All that time I was in hospital, and after. We look after each other, help each other. It's what friends do."

"I know that. But I felt I should just, you know ... say it out loud. Because it needs to be said."

"Sure," said Sharif. "But why now? What's up? Hold on. Don't tell me you've got cancer. You haven't, have you?"

"No."

"Phew. Then why?"

Tom almost told him. He almost started to explain about the Contest, the Lords of Pain, everything. He was sure it couldn't do any harm to share the truth with Sharif. Sharif could keep a secret, and anyway, if things went badly for Tom, a week from now the whole world would be under the rule of the Lord of Fire. The fact that demons were real would hardly be a secret *then*, would it?

But somehow Tom couldn't bring himself to say any of this. Sharif should be spared from knowing the terrible truth, at least for one more week. Besides, Tom was going to defeat the Lord of Fire. Wasn't he?

"No real reason," Tom said. "I'm in that kind of mood, that's all."

"OK, well, if we're done with all the hugs and kisses stuff," Sharif said, "any ideas what we should do after we've had our coffees?"

"I think I'd better head back, as a matter of fact. Got a few things I need to sort out."

"Sure. OK. Me too."

They parted. Tom walked home slowly along the heath's paths. Joggers thudded past him. Mothers and nannies pushed prams. Old people sat on benches, reading or just gazing around. On the grassy areas, people threw sticks and balls for their dogs. A few young couples lay on the ground, snogging. The day had begun to warm up, the sun trying to elbow through the clouds.

Tom felt something inside him start to loosen, a knot coming undone. For the first time since his duel on the Greek island, he began to understand what the Contest was really about again. He saw that he didn't need to beat Dragon just because he wanted to get his own back on him. He needed to beat Dragon because the world was counting on him to do so. All these people out on the heath, doing their everyday things, living their everyday lives, were counting on him. Tom was their knight in shining armour, their only hope, even if they had no way of knowing it. Without him, they were doomed.

His mother was right. It had done him good to get out here. Because now Tom knew, once more, what he was fighting for.

Not just himself. For everyone. For the people on the heath. For everyone on the planet, all six billion of them.

And as he walked, a plan began to form in Tom's mind.

It was a good plan. But he'd need help to pull it off.

Help that only two people he knew could provide.

Chapter 4
At the Airport

Mai and Great-aunt Akiko flew over from Japan two days later.

Tom and his mother met them at Heathrow Airport. Mai came out from the arrivals area first, shoving a trolley laden with baggage. She spotted Tom and speeded up, pushing the trolley at a run. As soon as she got to him, Mai went up on tiptoes and gave him a hug. Then she remembered to be more formal. She stepped back and bowed.

"True Warrior," she said, "I'm honoured to be able to help you at this time."

Tom returned the bow. "I'm honoured that you've come, Chop-socky Chick."

"Your poor face." Mai touched Tom's cheek and winced. "I didn't know the scars were so bad."

"I think they make me look cool. As if I've been in a fight or two."

"Maybe, yes. A little." Mai turned to Tom's mother. "Good afternoon, Jane Yamada," she said. She bowed very low. "I'm glad to meet you."

"Glad to meet you too, Mai," said Tom's mother. "Please, call me Aunt Jane. No, wait. That makes me sound so old. Just Jane will do."

"Of course," said Mai. "Jane."

Great-aunt Akiko bustled into view. Tom's mother pulled a face, as if she'd just smelled sour milk.

"Tomeo," said Great-aunt Akiko, placing her hands together and bowing. "Respected niece-in-law," she said to Tom's mother. This time she didn't bow. She bent her head forward just a little bit, but it wasn't a bow. It was hardly even a movement.

"Akiko," said Tom's mother.

"That's it?" Great-aunt Akiko huffed. "No proper greeting? No 'Akiko-san'?"

"Why bother? It's not as if we like each other."

"There is no harm in being polite. Have the English stopped being polite these days? We Japanese still are."

"Oh, I can be polite, don't you worry about that," Tom's mother said. "I just don't see why I should pretend I'm happy to see you. You're here because Tom needs you. That's the only reason I'm even talking to you."

The air between the two women sizzled with dislike.

"Perhaps, then, it would be better if you did not talk to me at all," said Great-aunt Akiko. "The last time you and I faced each other like this, after all, you were very rude to me. You called me a wrinkled old busy-body, and other much worse names. You said you were taking Tomeo away from Japan because you didn't trust me. You said I would try to interfere and bring up your son myself. You said I would spoil him. You acted in a quite shameful way. I have never been so insulted."

"It needed to be said," said Tom's mother, "and, for the record, I stand by every word of it. I knew what you were like, Akiko. I knew what you'd have done if I'd stayed in Japan. You'd have tried to tear Tom away from me. And I couldn't allow that. Especially with Ken dead. Ken would have stood beside me, against you. He'd have backed me up. Without him, I was all on my own, in a strange land. I didn't have any allies in Japan. It was just me on one side and the whole of the Yamada clan on the other. Getting out was the only sensible thing to do."

"But now you call on me," said Great-aunt Akiko. "Now you need me and the Yamada clan after all." She gave a smug little chuckle.

Tom's mother balled her hands into fists. She leaned over Great-aunt Akiko. Jane Yamada was nearly twice as tall as her. She towered over the little old woman.

"Listen, Akiko," she began.

Great-aunt Akiko looked up at her. She gave a slow, calm blink, and her small, black, spider-like eyes became very narrow. "Yes? Are you going to invent some new insult? I am not scared of you, Jane. Not at all."

"You *should* be scared," Tom's mother growled.

Tom knew he had to butt in. His mother was about to do something they would all regret.

"Ladies, ladies," he said, placing an arm between his mother and Great-aunt Akiko. "Let's stop this before it goes any further. Mum, back down. Picking a fight with Akiko isn't going to get us anywhere."

"But – "

"Mum, I'm serious. Leave it."

"Tom, how can you be on Akiko's side? You remember what she did to Sharif."

"I do, and I'm not on her side."

"She's an evil little troll."

Great-aunt Akiko hissed with outrage.

"That's as may be," Tom said. "But right now we have other stuff to think about. Much more important stuff. This is no time to argue or be rude. We need to work together. We

30

need Akiko. We need her help. And that means you have to bottle up your feelings about her and be nice, and so do I."

"Quite," said Great-aunt Akiko.

"The same goes for you, Grandmother," said Mai to Great-aunt Akiko. "I love you, you know that. But we are guests of my cousin and aunt, and we all have a shared aim. So you must behave too."

Great-aunt Akiko was shocked. Mai had never spoken to her like that before.

"Child, you would do well to remember your place," she said. "I am an elder of the family. You may not tell me what to do."

"Tom is right," Mai went on boldly. "We're here to work together. You must forget what happened all those years ago. The past is past. We must think about the future. We must do all we can to make sure there *is* a future."

Great-aunt Akiko thought this over. Then she turned her mouth down at the corners as a sign that she wasn't happy.

"Very well," she said. She looked at Tom's mother. "I forgive you, Jane, for your past rudeness."

"How very kind and generous of you," Tom's mother replied in an icy tone.

"And I hope that you and I might become friends."

"Don't hold your breath," Tom's mother muttered.

"Mum," warned Tom.

"OK, OK," his mother sighed. "I hope we might become friends too," she said to Great-aunt Akiko.

The two women shook hands without looking at each other.

"Excellent!" said Tom. "Fantastic!"

Tom knew that the truce he had just won was fragile at best. But it was better than nothing. He grabbed hold of the baggage trolley and headed for the car park.

Chapter 5
The Bank

As they drove into London on the M4, Great-aunt Akiko asked to be taken to see the Element Gems.

"Why?" said Tom's mother.

"I wish to look at them very closely. The Lord of Fire's gem should have started to fade by now. That will tell us how much time we have left to get ready for the next duel."

"We already know how much time we have, Akiko. Two days, three at most."

"Even so. I would like to see them. Please."

The word "please" sounded odd coming from Great-aunt Akiko. Tom had the feeling she didn't use it very often. She had to force it out of her mouth, with great effort.

Tom's mother looked at the clock on the car's dash-board. "The bank closes in less than an hour. We should be able to make it if the traffic's not too bad."

They got there with ten minutes to spare. Mr Loftus, the bank's weedy little senior manager, took them down in the lift to the vault below.

"Don't be too long," Mr Loftus said in his high squeaky voice. He shut the chamber door, sealing them in.

Tom's mother fetched out the black wooden box that held the Element Gems. She opened the lid. Tom, Mai and Great-aunt Akiko crowded round to look inside the box.

The fiery red Element Gem had indeed begun to fade. It looked see-through and fragile, as if it might shatter if someone touched it – if someone even so much as breathed on it.

"The Lord of Fire is a deadly enemy," Great-aunt Akiko said. "He is the most dangerous of the Five Lords of Pain, without any question. But now that he has their powers as well as his ..." She shuddered. "It is terrifying to think about."

She picked up one of the four other gems. It was the black one, the Lord of the Void's. She held the gem up to the light and looked at it through half-closed eyes.

"And this is one of the copies Dragon gave you?" she said. "Yes. I can see clearly how false it is. It looks the way an Element Gem should look. It could pass for the real thing, I suppose. But it does not give off any sense of power. Nor is there any light inside. This is just some kind of glass ball, that is all. A simple fake. And yet both of you were taken in by it."

"Grandmother," said Mai. "Behave. Remember?"

"What am I doing wrong?" said Great-aunt Akiko. "I am simply stating a fact. Tom and his mother should have known that these were not the real Element Gems, and, had they known that, they could have stopped Dragon sooner, before he gained the other Lords' powers."

Tom could see his mother was about to lose her temper again. She was pressing her lips tightly together to stop what she wanted to say coming out. He himself was finding it a strain not to let Great-aunt Akiko's mocking words get to him.

"We didn't have any reason to think they weren't the real thing, Great-aunt Akiko," he said. "It was the same every time. I handed

Dragon the gem, he slipped it into his pocket, then he handed it back to me a little later. I had no idea he'd swapped it with another gem. I wasn't on the look-out for anything like that. And I wasn't in the mood either. I'd just been through a fight with an arch-demon, don't forget. My life had been in danger. So checking if the gem that Dragon gave me was the real thing or not – it was hardly at the top of my list, was it?"

"Besides," said his mother, "an Element Gem doesn't glow just after it's been cut out of a Lord of Pain's heart. It takes a while for the power to build up inside it and for the glow to show through again. Till then, the gem does look pretty much like a 'glass ball', as you said, Akiko."

"I," said Great-aunt Akiko, "would never have been fooled. Not by this." She tossed the black gem into the air and caught it in one hand, showing how little she thought of it.

"Easy for you to say now, looking back," said Tom's mother. "But I wonder if you would really have noticed at the time."

"You doubt me? Are you calling me a liar?"

"I don't doubt that you *believe* what you're saying is the truth."

"Rude *gaijin* woman!" Great-aunt Akiko screamed. Her voice echoed loudly between the walls of the narrow chamber. "Insults again. Calling me a liar. How dare you?"

"And how dare you accuse me of being careless?" Tom's mother shouted back.

"I dare say that because you *were* careless."

"Stop!" Tom yelled at the top of his voice, louder than both of them. He tapped a T-shape with his hands. "Time out. I thought we agreed. No one is to argue. Keep it polite."

"And, Grandmother, *gaijin* is not a nice word," said Mai.

"It only means 'outsider'," said Great-aunt Akiko. "And she is an outsider."

"No, *gaijin* is always used in a rather nasty way in our country," Mai said. "It is a rude thing to say. You know that, and you know that Jane knows it too."

"Hmph," said Great-aunt Akiko. "All right, then. I apologise, Jane Yamada. I spoke without thinking."

"Apology accepted," said Tom's mother.

"And perhaps you should apologise to me."

"What for?"

"For not seeing that there was something wrong about Dragon. For hiring him as Tom's trainer. If not for that mistake, we would not be in the mess we are in now."

"It was a mistake, I admit," said Tom's mother. "But you can't blame me for it. Dragon hid his true nature well. How was I supposed to know he was really the Lord of Fire? It wasn't in any way clear. And it wasn't something any of the Lords of Pain had ever done before."

"And yet *I* understood that there was more to him than met the eye," said Great-aunt Akiko in a proud voice. "As soon as I saw him I knew."

"You didn't know he was the Lord of Fire," Mai pointed out.

"I knew he wasn't to be trusted."

"Well, we aren't always suspicious of everybody as you are, Akiko," said Tom's mother. "And the world would be a terrible place if we all were."

"Come *on*," said Tom. "Really. You're going too far. Much too far. Both of you. What's

41

done is done. We've all of us made mistakes. We've all been less than perfect – you included, Great-aunt Akiko. Now we have to move on. We're all Yamadas, and it's the Yamada family's job to beat the Lords of Pain. That's the only thing that matters. Or would you like the Lord of Fire to take over the earth? Is that what you want?

"No," said his mother.

"No," said Great-aunt Akiko.

"Good," said Tom. "At least we can all agree on that. So now – "

His mobile started to play its ringtone in his pocket, a clip of that old pop hit "Kung Fu Fighting".

"Blimey, I didn't think I could get a signal down here," he said.

The caller was Sharif. Tom flipped his phone open.

"Sharif, mate, bit busy right now. Can I call you back in half an hour?"

The mobile link was terrible. Sharif kept cutting out or getting drowned out by bursts of static. But there was no mistaking the fear in his voice. This must be urgent.

"Tom, listen, I'm ... *(crackle)* ... your house and there's ... *(crackle)* ... everywhere. The police have blocked off the whole road ... *(crackle)* ... see at least three ... *(crackle)* ... trying to put it out."

"What? Sharif, I can only just hear you. What's that about the house? Three what?"

"Three ... *(crackle)* ... engines. And I think ... *(crackle)* ... 20 fire fighters."

"Fire fighters?" said Tom. "Did you just say fire fighters?"

The colour drained from his mother's face.

"Yeah, fire fighters. The whole of ... *(crackle)* ... floor has gone up, Tom. It's ... *(crackle)* ... proper full-on blaze. Flames pouring ... *(crackle)* ... windows. You need to get ... *(crackle)* ... soon as you can."

"OK," said Tom. "All right. I'm on my way."

He snapped the phone shut.

"Mum ..."

"How bad, Tom?"

"I don't know. Bad, from the sound of it. Very bad."

Chapter 6
Fire

Blue lights spun and flashed, their beams bouncing off the sides of the houses. Three fire engines were parked in a row in the middle of the street. The roadway beneath their tyres was shiny with the water from their hose pipes. The smell of burning filled the early evening air.

Tom and his mother were at the end of the street, along with Sharif, Mai and Great-aunt Akiko. They were standing behind the strip of red-and-white *Fire and Rescue Service* tape which had been put up to hold back the crowds of onlookers and all the people who had been made to leave their nearby houses. They had been there for more than an hour.

The Watch Commander, who was directing the fire fighters, strode over to Tom's mother and her small group. His face was smudged with smoke.

"You're the owner of the property, am I right?" he said to Tom's mother. "You spoke to one of my officers earlier on. It's Mrs ... Yamaha, is it?"

"Yamada."

"Beg your pardon," said the Watch Commander. "Well, Mrs Yamada, the good news is the blaze is under control. We've put it out."

"What's the bad news?" asked Tom.

"Who are you?"

"I'm her son. It's my flat too."

46

"Well, I'm afraid it's been badly damaged," the Watch Commander told him.

"What does that mean?" said Tom's mother. "How badly?"

The Watch Commander took off his helmet. He had a very short haircut. He ran his hand back and forth across his scalp, scrubbing the stubble of his hair.

"I mean it's a write-off," he said. "The fire has gutted the place. We've gone in and had a good look round. It's a shambles. I'm truly sorry."

Jane Yamada struggled to hold back a sob. Her clothes, her furniture, everything she had – gone. Her photos of her husband too, and the gifts he had given her during their marriage. Everything else could be replaced, but not those.

"Was anyone hurt?" she asked.

"No," said the Watch Commander. "It was a lucky break. Someone from one of the flats below you smelled smoke and called us right away. By the time we got here, everyone was safely out of the building."

"Thank God. Do you have any idea how the fire started?"

"My best guess is that something went wrong with the electrical system. It's an old building. The wiring can be dodgy in places like that. A stray spark from a plug socket lands on the carpet or an armchair, can sit there slowly burning away for hours. Soon you've got a small flame, then something else catches alight ..." The Watch Commander spread out his hands. "And that's that."

"Can we go inside?" Tom asked.

"Not yet, young man. Not until we've made sure the whole house isn't going to fall down. You'd better try and find somewhere to stay for the night. For the next few nights, in fact. A friend's house, a hotel, somewhere like that."

"You and your mum can come and stay at my place, Tom," Sharif offered. He nodded at Mai and Great-aunt Akiko. "Them too. We'll make room for all of you."

"Thanks, Sharif," Tom said. "But your house is full up already."

"I'll get my sisters to give up their rooms. They can go and sleep in the garden shed!"

Tom smiled. "No, really, it's too much trouble. We'll find somewhere, don't worry."

Tom then turned to Great-aunt Akiko and fixed her with a long, hard stare. He wanted to say: *This is the kid you nearly killed with one of your Shinobi Ghosts. Now he's offered you a bed for the night, even though he's only just met you. I hope you feel bad.*

Great-aunt Akiko's spidery eyes gave away little. But Tom thought for a moment he did see a flicker of guilt in them.

The Watch Commander turned to go, then stopped. He fished inside one of the large pockets of his bulky jacket.

"Nearly forgot," he said, pulling out a tube-shaped object. "Something did survive the fire. One of my lads found it lying in the middle of the living room floor."

He was holding a parchment scroll, tied up with a red ribbon.

"Funny thing is," he went on, "everything inside the flat was burnt to a crisp apart from this. And it's made of paper. By rights it should be ashes like the rest. And yet there's not a mark on it. In 20 years with the fire brigade I've seen some rum sights, but this has to be the rummest."

Tom took the scroll from the Watch Commander.

"I hope it's of some value to you," the Watch Commander said. "Something that means a lot to you. A certificate maybe?"

"It's worth something," Tom said tight-lipped.

The Watch Commander gave a quick, hopeful grin.

"Well, that's good, then," he said. "I always say, if the victims of a fire can walk away with just one item that has been saved, then it hasn't been a total disaster. Eh? Am I right?"

"Yeah," said Tom, clutching the Lord of Fire's challenge to his chest. "You're spot-on."

Chapter 7
Fear

They booked into a chain hotel near the Royal Free Hospital. They took two rooms with a door between them. Tom would be sharing with his mother, Mai with Akiko.

They ordered supper from room service and ate together at the table in Tom's and his mother's suite. Tom was feeling numb inside. The shock of the fire was starting to sink in. He hardly tasted the food.

His mother saw his face and could tell what he was thinking.

"It's OK, Tom," she soothed. "We're fully insured against fire. We can get it all back. Your laptop, your Nintendo, your books, comics, DVDs, iPod, everything. And guess what? I'd been thinking for a while that the flat could do with a make-over. Everything was starting to look a bit old and tired. I had plans to get the living room and the bathroom painted anyway. Now I get the chance to do up the whole lot!"

She laughed, but her red-rimmed eyes told a different story.

"It won't be the same," Tom said.

"No, it won't," his mother agreed. "But it might be better, you never know."

"This was the Lord of Fire's doing," said Great-aunt Akiko with a sour look.

"Yeah," said Tom. "The other four Lords of Pain just broke one thing each when they sent their challenges. The table, the TV – nothing worse than that. Not Dragon, though. That's not enough for him. He has to go and trash the whole flat. Talk about overkill."

"He must really hate you," said Mai.

"I don't see why," Tom replied. "I mean, I can understand him looking down on me. That makes sense. To him, I'm a weakling and a fool. But hate me? To hate someone, you have to consider that person to be at least your equal. And Dragon, as far as I know, thinks I'm way beneath him."

"Maybe that's just it," said Mai. "Maybe he doesn't think you're beneath him. Maybe he does consider you an equal."

"Or, more than that, he thinks you're a threat," said Great-aunt Akiko. "Hate, after all, most often has its roots in fear."

Tom frowned at her. "Me? A threat? You're saying the Lord of Fire's scared of me?" He shook his head. "I don't think so."

"It's possible," said Great-aunt Akiko. "I believe the Lord of Fire has shown us something of his true nature by destroying your home. Yes, he wishes to remind you how powerful he is. But what he has also done, without meaning to, is tell us that he feels the need to boast and show off."

"He's not very confident!" said Tom's mother.

"That's just it."

"Like a rich man spending money on flashy cars and big houses. Because really he's just a small man inside and he wants to make the world pay attention to him."

"Not a bad comparison," said Great-aunt Akiko.

"What you're getting at, Akiko," said Tom's mother, "is that the Lord of Fire isn't as sure as he would like to be about winning the duel."

"That is what I would conclude," said Great-aunt Akiko. "Which is a good sign. It gives us cause for hope."

Tom looked at Mai. Mai looked back at him with wide eyes. Could this be? Tom's mother and Great-aunt Akiko talking to each other without arguing? Even making plans together? What next?

"Now, Tomeo," Great-aunt Akiko said. "The time has come to open that scroll and find out when and where the duel is to take place."

Tom undid the ribbon and unrolled the scroll. He was about to pass the scroll to his mother so that she could read the *kanji* words written inside. Then he changed his mind and passed it to Great-aunt Akiko instead. He thought she would be pleased to be asked. He glanced at his mother, and she nodded back.

Great-aunt Akiko took the scroll, saying, "*Domo arigato*, Tomeo."

She began studying the scroll. Tom felt Mai nudge him in his ribs.

Mai whispered, "Tom! My grandmother just said thank you."

"I know."

"She never says thank you to anyone!"

"I heard that, Mai," said Great-aunt Akiko gruffly.

"Well, it's true, isn't it?" said Mai.

Great-aunt Akiko didn't reply. At last she finished reading the scroll.

"The Lord of Fire has chosen a church as the site for the duel," she said.

"A church?" said Tom.

"A very large one. I know the proper word for it in English. I am just finding it hard to remember it."

"Cathedral?" Tom's mother suggested.

"Yes. A cathedral. In a place called Canterbury. That is not so far from here, I believe."

"Not far at all. It's down in Kent. Fifty miles or so."

"You must be there tomorrow night, at midnight," Great-aunt Akiko said.

"Tomorrow night," Tom said. "Halloween."

"A good night for demons."

"And he wants me to fight him in a cathedral. Is that proper? Is that allowed? He is a demon, after all, and a cathedral is holy ground. Does that make sense?"

"Churches, temples, stone circles, they're all places of magical power," said Tom's mother. "Most churches are built on sites which people have held to be holy for thousands of years, long before the birth of Christ. A sacred spot remains a sacred spot, whether there's a church on it, or a grove of trees, or a cave, or just nothing."

"Does this cathedral have a grave-yard?" Great-aunt Akiko asked.

"I think it must have," said Tom, "but I don't know for sure. I'd Google it for you, if I still had a laptop."

"I have my phone," said Mai. She took out a mobile from her Hello Kitty bag. Tom's eyes grew large. He'd never seen a phone like it. It was as thin as a credit card and as sleek as a dagger.

The phone also had voice recognition and an inboard AI system. Mai switched it on simply by saying her name: "Mai Yamada".

"*Konnichiwa*, Mai," said the phone in a low, flirty voice like a teenage boy's. It asked a question in Japanese. Mai replied, and in an instant the phone had linked her up to the internet. It asked another question, Mai answered, and a moment later the phone was looking for information on Canterbury Cathedral.

"That's amazing," Tom said. "We don't have phones anywhere near as clever as that over here. Must be brand new, right?"

"Oh, no, this is old," said Mai. "I've had it at least a year. It takes ages to do anything, and I'm going to upgrade it to something faster as soon as I can."

"Still, makes me proud to be half-Japanese," Tom said. "Not that I wasn't proud already," he added, for Great-aunt Akiko's benefit.

Mai read facts about the cathedral off the phone's screen.

"Founded in 602 AD," she said. "Rebuilt after the Norman invasion of Britain. And again in the fifteenth century, in the Gothic style. Pilgrims flocked there in the Middle Ages. The Germans tried to bomb it during the

Second World War but missed." She spoke to the phone. Text scrolled down across the screen. "And yes, it does have a grave-yard. On the north side."

Great-aunt Akiko didn't quite smile. Tom didn't think she was able to. But, the wrinkles on either side of her mouth seemed to get deeper.

"Excellent," she said.

She drew herself up and stood as tall as she could, which wasn't very high.

"I have things to do now," she said. "Tomeo, you must get all the sleep you can. Mai, you as well. It would perhaps be a good idea, Mai, if you moved into the other room with your cousin and his mother. I have a busy night ahead, and my work will cause rather a lot of disturbance. Goodnight."

Great-aunt Akiko bustled out of the room.

Tom offered Mai his bed, but she insisted on using the sofa.

"You are the Contest champion," she said. "You deserve a proper bed."

Tom slept in fits and starts. All night long he dreamed about fighting Dragon. Sometimes he was winning, sometimes losing. Several times he woke up to hear noises coming from the other next room. Great-aunt Akiko was chanting in her rough, scratchy voice. Tom saw lights flickering in the gap under the door. *Candle flames*, he thought. There was also a strong smell that leaked through into the room. It was like joss-sticks, thick and sweet and sickly.

Great-aunt Akiko was working her magic.

Would it be enough to help him? Would it make a difference?

Tom didn't know.

Chapter 8
Last Things

Tom got up at dawn. He cleared an area of floor in the hotel room and began doing his exercises.

His mother was snoring softly in her bed. Mai lay on the sofa, half covered by a blanket. She was snoring too. Daylight glowed grey behind the curtains.

Tom went through all the *kata* routines he knew. He shifted from position to position, swiftly, gently, in silence. He tuned in to his body. He felt his muscles working. He felt the blood pulsing through his veins. He listened to his heartbeat. He breathed in and out, slow and steady. Spirit and flesh became one.

A voice kept speaking in his mind, telling him what to do. It was Dragon's voice. It was always there when Tom practised his *kata*. When he did anything to do with martial arts. Tom had got used to hearing Dragon's commands during seven years of training with him. Now Dragon's voice continued to echo in his head, even though Dragon was no longer his *sensei*. Tom couldn't shut it up. All he could do was try to take no notice.

When he finished his *kata*, he had a shower. He turned the water up to as hot as he could bear. He stood there for fifteen minutes, letting the burning needles of water stab down on him. This could be the last shower he ever took.

He got dressed. His mother and Mai were still asleep. He went downstairs to the hotel dining room and had breakfast. He ate his bacon and eggs slowly. He ordered an extra round of toast. He drank his coffee in small sips. This could be the last breakfast he ever ate.

He went outside. He strolled down the road, looking in all the shop windows. The only shop that was open this early was a newsagent's. Tom bought a paper. He sat and read it on a bench outside a Starbucks. The paper was full of doom and gloom, as always. Football stars were cheating on their wives, MPs were cheating the tax payer. This could be the last newspaper he ever read.

In the end, he took out his mobile and phoned Debbie. It wasn't likely that she would be awake at this time of day. But Tom didn't really want to talk to her. He just wanted to leave her a message.

"Hi, Debbie," he said to her voice-mail. "It's Tom. Tom Yamada. You know, the guy you may think has been avoiding you. You gave my mum your mobile number, so I guess you want me to call you. Or you don't mind if I call you, at any rate. So here I am. Calling you."

He paused.

"And now that I *am* calling you," he said, "I'm not sure what to say. Just that I'm sorry if you've got the idea that I don't like you. I do. I really do. I've had some stuff I've had to take care of, that's all. I can't tell you what. If I did, I'd have to kill you. Ha ha. That's a joke, by the way. Not a very funny one, I know. Sorry."

Get a grip, Tom told himself. *Stick to the point.*

"Listen, Debbie," he said. "This is how it is. Today's Halloween. Tomorrow, I'll be calling you again. I hope. If I do – no, when I do – I'd like to ask you out. On a date. Whatever you want us to do is fine with me. See a movie, go for a meal, just hang out at Camden Market or somewhere, whatever, I don't mind. Except, if

66

it's a movie, please not a chick flick. I get plenty of those at home with my mum. I'd just like to spend some time with you. You're a great girl and you're dead pretty. Most of all with your glasses on. But also without them. Not that there's anything wrong with wearing glasses. Oh, God, I'm making a right mess of this, aren't I?"

Yeah, he thought, *you're ace at playing the romantic lover, Tom.*

"Just ... give me a chance," he said. "I mean another chance. Please, Debbie. By tomorrow, nothing will be the same. I won't be the same. You'll see."

He switched off the phone. He sat for a while with the mobile pressed against his cheek. Then he stood up and walked back to the hotel.

By now, his mother and Mai were up and dressed.

"There you are," his mother said as Tom entered the room. "I was wondering where you'd got to. I was starting to get worried."

"Just enjoying the morning," Tom said. "Making the most of it. What, did you think I'd run off or something?"

"Tom wouldn't run off," said Mai. "He's no coward. He's a True Warrior."

Great-aunt Akiko came in. She was wearing one of the hotel's white bathrobes. It looked huge on her, as if she'd been swallowed by a polar bear.

"It is done," Great-aunt Akiko said. She looked pale and worn out. "Everything is ready. Now there is nothing to do but wait."

The day crawled by. Tom and Mai talked martial arts routines, in between watching a lot of TV. Great-aunt Akiko had found green tea on sale at a nearby supermarket, and she brewed endless cups of it for them all. Tom's mother made phone calls to the insurance people and also to the bank she worked for in the City. She told her boss about the fire at the flat and asked for a few days' leave so that she could sort things out. Her boss was very understanding and told her to take as much time off as she needed.

Afternoon came. Outside, a thin, drizzly rain began to fall, but it didn't last long. *Just a few hours to go now*, Tom thought. A few hours till he faced his greatest ever battle. It was odd how calm he felt. *I should be in a panic*, he thought. But somehow the idea of facing the Lord of Fire didn't scare him any more. In a weird way he was looking forward to the fight. Soon it would all be over – the Contest would be settled one way or the other. His whole life had been moving towards this moment. This was his last day as Contest champion. Tomorrow, he would be just an ordinary boy. He'd have nothing more to worry about other than the usual stuff –

school, girls, what music was cool and what wasn't, that sort of thing.

Tom could almost count himself lucky. His father had had to wait 30 years before he could finish with being champion (and he'd never got the chance to enjoy what came after, poor man). The same with all the first-born Yamada sons who had gone before. It had been 30 years before they could start to lead a normal life.

For Tom, it was just fifteen years.

That was a real bonus.

Tomorrow would be more than just a new day for Tom. It would be a whole new start.

If, of course, he was still alive after tonight.

A big if.

Chapter 9
The Cathedral

They drove down to Kent just as it was getting dusk. Tom was already wearing his combat *gi*. So was Mai. And the boot of the car was loaded with the weapons which Mai and Great-aunt Akiko had brought over with them from Japan.

Everywhere in London kids were out and about, trick-or-treating. The streets were filled with people dressed as skeletons, ghosts, witches, vampires, superheroes and fairies, all of them carrying bags stuffed with sweets.

It was the same in Canterbury. As Tom stepped out of the car, he felt that nobody was paying him any attention. Or Mai either. In their combat *gi* they were just two more young people in costume. Tonight, of all nights, they looked like everyone else. They blended in.

Canterbury Cathedral was a huge, proud building. Its three towers rose high above the rooftops of the smaller buildings all round it. Each of the towers had four spires which pointed up to heaven like the arms of people praying.

Flood-lights lit up the cathedral on all sides, so that it seemed to shine against the backdrop of the dark night sky. You had to admire how much effort must have gone into building something so enormous and so beautiful, back in the days before modern tools made jobs of this kind far easier. Every block of stone had had to be carried here from somewhere else, carved to the right shape, and hoisted up into place by hand. The time it must have taken! The number of people involved!

As he drew near to the cathedral, Tom looked up. Ugly stone faces jutted out round the edge of the roof. Gargoyles. They were there to spit out the rainwater from the gutter. They peered down with their eyes bulging, their mouths grinning and their tongues lolling out. They were statues of monsters, and they made Tom think of the demons who would be watching tonight's duel. The Contest legend said that people went on remembering how demons looked, long after demons had been banished from this world. These gargoyles were the proof.

The cathedral had a pair of huge wooden doors at its main entrance. They were firmly shut and locked. A sign said that visitors were welcome between the hours of nine and five. It was now seven p.m.

"How are we supposed to get in?" Tom asked.

"The Lord of Fire will see to that," said Great-aunt Akiko. "At midnight, this place will become his. A building much like this one stands in his world where the cathedral stands in ours. The two will merge when the time comes for the duel to begin. The Lord of Fire will let you in."

"Oh," said Tom.

"The final duel of a Contest always takes place in a great building," Great-aunt Akiko said. "Your father fought the Lord of the Typhoon at the Budokan in Tokyo."

Tom looked blank.

"The Budokan's an arena," Mai explained. "They hold sumo wrestling contests there. And art shows. Concerts too. I saw Westlife there once, a while back. They rocked!"

Westlife? thought Tom. *Westlife rocked?*

"Do you like Westlife, Tom?" Mai asked.

"Um, not my thing, really," Tom said. "Mum does. Don't you, Mum?"

His mother blushed. "My secret vice," she said.

"Which bands do you like, then?" Mai asked Tom.

"All sorts," Tom replied. "Indie stuff most of the time. A bit of hip-hop too. Nothing that really gets into the charts."

"You must send me some files over the internet."

"Sure. OK. But be warned, none of what I like sounds anything like Westlife. It's about as unlike Westlife as you can get."

"If you like it, I'm sure I'll like it," said Mai.

"Are we really standing here talking about music?" Tom said, amazed. "When we're just about to battle the Lord of Fire?"

"We've got to talk about something, haven't we?" said Mai. "To pass the time. Might as well be music."

"Well, yes ... but ... It's just odd. The world could end tonight. Next to that, it doesn't seem important what sort of music someone does or doesn't like."

"But that's what we're here for, Tom," Mai said. "We're fighting to save the world so that there can be more music. And not only music. More of all the things that make people happy and glad to be alive. Art. Books. Movies. Computer games. The things that make life worth living."

"Like Westlife?"

"Yes!" said Mai, clapping her hands. "Of course Westlife!"

Tom sighed and rolled his eyes. "Oh, well. If we *have* to."

Chapter 10
Midnight

Long, cold hours passed. The cathedral's bell tolled eight, nine, ten ...

At last midnight was at hand.

Great-aunt Akiko stood ready. She had a large china bowl, which she laid on the ground outside the cathedral door. Into the bowl she poured a clear, sweet-smelling liquid from a flask. She stirred the liquid seven times anti-clockwise with a wooden whisk. Then she took out a small glass tube full of white powder. She pulled out the tube's cork stopper and tapped out the powder into the liquid. She stirred it again, at the same time muttering under her breath in Japanese.

The liquid in the bowl turned cloudy, then started to froth and bubble. Smoke arose from its surface in twisting, swirling strands. The smoke began to drift sideways. It headed towards the north side of the cathedral, sliding through the air like snakes of vapour. Tom noticed that there was a slight breeze – but it was blowing in the opposite direction, to the south.

The smoke was travelling *against* the breeze, not with it.

Tom felt goosebumps prickling all over him.

Magic.

Then the cathedral clock struck twelve.

The sound of the bell changed. At first it was the same deep, clanging *bong* Tom had been hearing all evening. With every stroke of the hour, however, the *bongs* became harsher, more shrill. Soon each was more like a scream than a chime. The last of them howled out across the rooftops, its echo travelling far into the darkness of the night.

Silence followed, a terrible hush. It seemed as if all of Canterbury was holding its breath. All of the world, even.

Then there was a loud *boom* from inside the cathedral. The doors shook. Then they slowly started to open. Each of them swung inwards, to reveal a curtain of shimmering mist, shot through with rainbow glimmers.

Tom turned to Mai. Both he and she were loaded up with weapons. They were like walking adverts for all things sharp and deadly.

"All set?" he asked.

Mai gulped and nodded. It was the first time Tom had ever seen her scared.

"All set," she said.

"We can do this," Tom said.

"I know."

Tom looked back at his mother. Mai looked back at her grandmother.

Then, side by side, the two of them stepped through the door of the cathedral, through the curtain of shimmering mist.

Chapter 11
The Lord of Fire

What lay on the other side of the cathedral doorway wasn't the image that Tom had seen on the screen of Mai's phone. It wasn't stained-glass windows, and rows of wooden seating. And it wasn't high arched roofs, tall pillars, and gleaming brass candlesticks, going back for a hundred metres and more.

No, where Tom and Mai were now wasn't Canterbury Cathedral. Not by a long shot. It was some place quite else.

There were stone benches arranged in a huge horseshoe shape. They rose one above the other, piled up all the way to a dome-shaped roof a hundred metres up. All of them overlooked a large area with a stone floor. There were five thrones lined up side by side, just in front of this central space. And there were demons, thousands of them, filling the tiers of stone benches. They were looking down with bulging eyes like the gargoyles outside. A vast number of brightly coloured many-eyed creatures with scales and wings and horns. They were all chattering to one another in an excited way. Everything was lit by clusters of round lanterns that gave off a bright yellow light.

The noise of the demon voices grew louder as they saw Tom and Mai come in through the misty curtain.

It wasn't far to the centre of the arena but it felt like miles. The demons howled and booed Tom and Mai all the way. Tom didn't remember the demons being nearly as lively as this during the four duels he'd fought before. It must be because they knew how powerful the Lord of Fire now was. No Lord of Pain had ever seemed more likely to defeat the Contest champion. The demons felt that victory was truly within their grasp. The earth was as good as theirs.

Tom and Mai kept going till they reached the five thrones. The thrones were empty. They were all made of gold but their seats were covered in different colours of velvet. One was grey, one was black, one was blue and one was green. The middle one was red.

Tom and Mai waited. The demons went on yelling at them.

"Any idea what they're saying to us?" Mai asked.

"I don't speak demon language," said Tom. "But put it this way. I don't think they're telling us how wonderful we are."

All of a sudden the hullabaloo died down. The demons started shushing and whispering to one another.

Someone had walked in from a doorway set behind the thrones, at the base of the stone benches.

It was the Lord of the Mountain.

The huge, fat arch-demon limped across to the thrones. He sat down heavily on the one with the grey velvet seat. He scowled at Tom.

"I've been looking forward to this, Yamada," he said in a raspy growl. "You took my head off. I'm hoping the Lord of Fire will take off yours."

Then a second arch-demon popped into view. It was the Lord of the Void. His black armour clanked as he took his seat next to the Lord of the Mountain.

"May the Lord of Fire beat you to death," he said to Tom.

Third to come out was the Lord of Tears.

"Sneaky little rat," he snarled at Tom. He glanced at Mai. "And you've brought your useless side-kick along too. How sweet. Not that it'll help you any."

The fourth Lord of Pain arrived. The Lord of the Typhoon flew down from above, gliding to a halt by the thrones. He folded his wings behind his back as he sat down. One of his wings, the one Tom had slashed during their duel, wouldn't close properly. It stuck out at an odd angle.

"The Lord of Fire will kill you," he told Tom. "But it would please me if he crippled you first, as you crippled me."

"Yeah, yeah, yeah," said Tom. By now he'd had enough of the four Lords of Pain and the trash-talking. "You don't bother me. I beat you all. The only thing I'm hearing here is the whines of a sad bunch of losers."

Mai laughed. Some of the demons in the audience giggled too.

That told Tom something. The demons didn't respect these four Lords of Pain any more. The four arch-demons had lost their power to command.

And Tom thought he knew why.

The demons had decided to pin all their hopes on the Lord of Fire. They were loyal to him, because he stood every chance of winning a Contest at last. The demons were not a brave crowd. They liked the idea of a single strong leader, someone they could safely follow. The Lord of Fire was that leader.

Tom's guess was proved correct a moment later, when the Lord of Fire himself entered. As he strode in a great cheer went up. The demons hooted and yelled with delight to see him. The noise was horrific.

The Lord of Fire walked up to the middle of the five thrones. He didn't sit down, however. He stood, drinking in the demons' loud acclaim. He raised his arms in a grand manner, like an athlete on the winners' stand or a rock star at the end of a show. He grinned a sharp-toothed grin.

Tom studied him. The Lord of Fire wasn't very tall. He didn't look very strong either. He had bright scarlet skin. He had a ring of horns round the top of his head like a crown. His eyes were like twin flames. He had a tail with a pointed tip. He had red, bat-like wings.

Tom could see Dragon in him. The shape of his face was the same as Dragon's. He had the same bald-topped head. He held himself in the same way.

But Dragon had been a man, or at least had looked like one. The Lord of Fire was pure demon. This red creature was what had been hiding inside Dragon all along. It was Dragon's true face.

At last the cheering ended. The last echoes of it faded out somewhere up high near the domed ceiling.

The Lord of Fire spoke.

"What a glorious night this is," he said to the demons. His voice roared like a furnace. "I thank you all for coming. Truly, this is going to be our night. A night that has been far too long in coming. You all know what has happened, why things are different now. You know what I've done. I've been away. I've spent the past fifteen years out there in the human world. I pretended to be one of them, a human. I hatched a splendid plan. I trained the latest Contest champion. Can you believe that? I, the Lord of Fire, had the job of teaching a first-born Yamada son how to fight!"

The watching demons thought this was very funny. The air was filled with their jabbering laughter.

"And not only that," the Lord of Fire went on, "I used him. I used him against my fellow Lords of Pain. I gave him just the right skills to defeat each of them, then tricked him into handing me their Element Gems. He gave the gems to me, after he took them from the other Lords. He had no idea what he was doing. And here they are."

The Lord of Fire pointed to a necklace he was wearing. It was made of thin gold chain, and the four Element Gems were strung along it in a row. The gems pulsed with a soft, steady light.

"Now I have the powers of my fellow Lords of Pain," he said. "Powers which, trust me, I will make good use of."

The other four Lords of Pain glared at the Lord of Fire from their thrones. There was shame and hatred in their eyes. There was longing, too. Longing for the gems that hung around the Lord of Fire's neck. A hunger that hurt.

"Look at them now!" the Lord of Fire crowed. He waved a hand at the four Lords of Pain. "Look! Weak. Miserable. Beaten. Cheated. Have you ever seen a sadder sight?"

The demons jeered at the four Lords of Pain on their thrones. They made mocking faces and hooting ape-like noises.

The four Lords of Pain scowled. They ground their teeth. But that, it seemed, was all they could do.

"What are they now, without their Element Gems?" said the Lord of Fire. "Nothing! Arch-demons? No, just demons. No better than any of you. I am the only true arch-demon left."

He pounded his chest.

"That means I am the only one fit to rule you. It is I who will lead you out into the human world before this night is over. I who will bring you what you have waited for, yearned for, all these thousands of years. To win at last! Victory!"

The Lord of Fire turned. He looked down at Tom.

"And all that stands between us and our prize," he said, "is this. This small, ugly, scared little boy."

He looked at Mai.

"Oh, and the tiny friend he's decided to bring along with him. A mascot of some kind. You would think so, by the size of her. But in fact, she's another member of the Yamada clan. It's clear that the boy thinks she will be of some help to him. She won't. I will fight her as well, even though nowhere in the rules does it state that I have to. Destroy one Yamada, destroy two – it's all the same to me. In fact, I consider it a bargain. Two for the price of one. A double deal. Double duel, you might say."

He chuckled, pleased by the play on words.

"It might take me a few moments longer to finish off both of them, but so what? It'll be extra fun for you all to watch. And then, quite soon, this will all be over. This joke they call a Contest will be at an end. No longer will we be the outcasts in this miserable world. Soon we will – "

"Oh, for heaven's sake!" Tom exploded. "You always were in love with the sound of your own voice, Dragon. Why don't you just give it a rest? These demons haven't come here to listen to you flap your lips all night. They're here for a show. So let's give them one."

The Lord of Fire grinned, but it was more of a sneer than a smile.

"Very well, Tom," he said. "I see you've come armed to the teeth, both of you. I myself will not be using any weapons. Why would I need to? I have five Element Gems."

He touched the necklace.

"I feel their power rushing through me. It fills me like a stormy sea. My blood sings with it. So strong! So swift! So supple! Thanks to them, I can now do *this*."

He stamped his foot. Tom and Mai were shaken about and thrown onto their knees.

"And *this*."

The Lord of Fire vanished from sight with a *shwoop*. He popped back into view just behind Tom and Mai, who were still reeling from his stamp. He cuffed Tom on the side of the head with his right hand, Mai with his left.

"And *this*."

He stretched himself like toffee through the gap between Tom and Mai. Then he spun and seized them both by the throat.

"Not to mention *this*."

He took off, hauling Tom and Mai into the air. Ten feet up, he let go. Tom and Mai dropped to the floor, landing hard. Weapons fell off them, clattering onto the flagstones.

The Lord of Fire came back down.

"And of course," he said, "not that you've seen it before – *this*."

He opened his mouth wide. Tom glimpsed a glowing light at the back of his throat. Then a jet of flame burst out from his mouth, shooting towards Tom and Mai.

They scrambled out of the way. They just avoided getting scorched. They got to their feet, both of them stunned and dazed by the Lord of Fire's five-part attack.

The Lord of Fire cocked his head. "Had enough yet, children?" he asked.

Tom drew his *katana*.

Mai unhooked a pair of *kama* sickles from her belt.

"Here's your answer," Tom said. "*Banzai!*"

Mai took up the cry. "*Banzai!*"

Together, they charged at the Lord of Fire.

Chapter 12
Double Duel

Tom aimed high. Mai aimed low. Tom swung his sword at the Lord of Fire's neck. Mai slashed at his legs.

The Lord of Fire ducked and jumped at the same time. He flew under the *katana* and over the sickles. Next instant, with a *shwoop*, he vanished.

Tom and Mai wheeled round, scanning for him all around the arena.

Shwoop.

The Lord of Fire popped back into view above them. He swooped, with his wings flattened against his back, in a sharp nose-dive, breathing fire as he came.

Tom rolled to the left, Mai to the right. But Mai was a fraction too slow. The jet of fire struck the floor and spread outwards. Flames licked Mai's foot. Her shoe was on fire.

"Mai!" Tom yelled.

Mai slapped at the flames to put them out. When that didn't work she kicked the shoe off her foot.

Too late. Her foot had been scorched. From toe to ankle the skin was blistered and red.

The Lord of Fire landed beside her. He grabbed her foot and gave it a hard, nasty squeeze.

"I think that must hurt a lot," he said.

"Not as much as this is going to hurt!" Mai shot back. She lashed out at his knee with one of her sickles.

The Lord of Fire made his leg go bendy, as if it was made of rubber. It flopped backwards in a way that no normal leg could. The sickle missed his knee by a long way.

He fixed his attention back on Mai's foot.

"Maybe it would help if I burned your foot off altogether," he said. "Don't worry, you won't bleed to death. The burning will seal the wound."

"Do your worst, *baka*," spat Mai.

"Bad girl," said the Lord of Fire. "Such rude talk from such a sweet-looking young lady. Seems I need to burn your tongue out as well."

He opened his jaws as wide as they could go.

A *shuriken* went *thunk* into his arm.

"Hey!" said Tom. "Remember me?"

The Lord of Fire turned.

"Like I could forget," he growled. "The stupid brat I've had to put up with for seven years." He plucked the throwing-star out of his arm and tossed it aside. The blood that oozed out from the wound glowed bright orange, like lava. "Not a bad shot, Tom. But I bet you were trying to hit somewhere else. My head, maybe."

Yes, thought Tom. "No," he said.

"Your lying is as poor as your aim," said the Lord of Fire.

Shwoop.

All at once he was right in front of Tom.

He slammed his hand, palm flat, into Tom's chest.

Tom went flying backwards. He crashed against the Lord of the Void's throne. The Lord of the Void gave him a kick, shoving him back into the arena.

Tom rolled over into a crouch. He looked at the four seated Lords of Pain. An idea came to him.

"Are you just going to let the Lord of Fire do this?" he taunted them. "Are you going to let him use your powers? He was one of you once. Doesn't it make you feel dumb, the way he stole your Element Gems from you? The way he's set himself up as the one and only leader of all the demons? That's got to hurt, hasn't it? That's got to be eating you guys up inside."

The Lord of Tears shook his head. The Lord of the Mountain looked away. The Lord of the Typhoon let out an angry grunt.

"We'll still get to attack your world," the Lord of Void said from behind the visor of his helmet. "We'll still be part of the army that destroys your lands and enslaves your race."

"But you'll be followers, not leaders," Tom said. "You'll be no better than slaves yourselves. His slaves."

The four Lords of Pain shifted about on their thrones. They grumbled angrily.

"Not quite fair, is it?" Tom said. "Not what you'd been hoping for, after all this time. So why don't you rise up and turn on him. Together, all four of you, I know you could – "

A hand gripped the back of Tom's head. It held on so tight, that Tom could hear the bones of his skull start to creak.

"What's going on here?" said the Lord of Fire. His voice was loud, his mouth right beside Tom's ear. "Having a little chat with the other Lords, Tom? Those four aren't worth a moment of your time. They're fools. Always have been, always will be. I can't believe I put up with them for so long. I can't believe I ever thought of them as my equals. I should have stolen their powers ages ago. They didn't deserve to have them in the first place ... I hope you don't feel too much at ease sitting on those thrones," he said to the four Lords. "Enjoy them while you can. It'll be the last time anyone will treat you with respect."

With that, he flung Tom backwards by the head. Tom flew through the air again, this time for what seemed like several seconds. Finally he hit the floor. He rolled over and over till he came to a stop, in a heap.

Tom tried to stand. He felt battered and woozy, as if he'd just been in a bad car crash. Everything swam in front of his eyes. The world wobbled out of focus.

He saw Mai – it had to be Mai – lunging at the Lord of Fire. She was lashing out with a *chigiriki*. She was also dragging her burnt foot, and so not moving as fast as she'd normally have been able to.

The Lord of Fire – the red, man-shaped blur that was the Lord of Fire – turned round. He snatched hold of the *chigiriki's* chain, just next to the spiked metal cylinder on the end. He yanked on the chain. Mai was caught off-guard and was dragged towards him. The Lord of Fire took hold of a handful of her hair. Then he began hitting her hard in the face with his fist. He punched her again and again, without let-up, without mercy.

Tom knew he had to go and help Mai. But since when had it become so hard to stand up? It was as if the air was solid and his limbs were made of jelly.

The Lord of Fire kept hitting Mai. Her whole body jerked with every blow.

Tom thought of Great-aunt Akiko. What was keeping her? Her part of the plan should have been put into action by now. She'd better get a move on.

Otherwise, Mai was dead.

Chapter 13
March of the Ninjas

Outside the cathedral, Jane Yamada waited and worried. She wished she could see what was happening inside. But she was stopped by the hazy curtain that stood across the two doorways.

Akiko was still busy chanting her magic. She had her eyes shut. The spell fell from her lips. She was speaking Japanese, but a very old form of Japanese. Jane had never heard of half the words. From what she could gather, Akiko was addressing the spirits of the dead. She was saying how much she hated to disturb their rest but she needed their aid.

The china bowl was now empty. All of the liquid had turned to vapour and wafted off round the side of the cathedral.

All at once, Akiko stopped chanting. Her eyes snapped open.

"They have risen," she said. "They are coming."

Jane Yamada felt a tingle of fear crawl across her scalp. She had some dim idea what to expect now. That didn't mean she wanted to see it very much.

First she heard shuffling footsteps coming from round the corner.

Next, a figure lurched into view.

It was the size and shape of a person. But it wasn't a person. Or rather, it hadn't been one for a very long time.

It was a skeleton.

A collection of crumbling brown bones.

It came towards Jane and Akiko, step by uneven step. Its skull stared with empty black eye sockets. Its teeth grinned like piano keys. Its joints clicked and rattled.

Akiko clamped a claw-like hand on Jane's wrist.

"Don't move," she hissed. "Move, and you may startle it and it may attack. Let it go past you. It and all the others."

Jane did as she was told, even though what she really wanted to do was scream and run away.

More skeletons came stumping round the corner. Many of them had tatters of clothing still clinging to them. Clumps of soil fell off them as they walked. They had clawed their way up out of their graves.

As they got closer, Jane saw that each of the skeletons was trailing smoke. It was the same smoke that had come from the bowl.

And before her eyes, the smoke began to draw itself round the skeletons. It wrapped them up tightly, like bandages on a mummy. Then it grew thick and solid. It became a kind of white flesh. Then it became more than that. It became skin. And eyes. And faces. And clothing. And weapons.

All at once the skeletons were men.

Ninjas.

Shinobi Ghosts.

The Shinobi Ghosts tramped past Jane and Akiko in a line. There were dozens of them, perhaps as many as 50 in all. They strode towards the curtain of shimmering mist that hung across the cathedral entrance.

Jane knew that nothing living could pass through that barrier.

But of course, the Shinobi Ghosts *weren't* living.

One after another the ninjas vanished through the shimmering whiteness, into the cathedral.

As the last of them went in, Akiko swayed and groaned.

"Feel ... faint," she gasped.

She would have fallen if Jane Yamada hadn't caught her in time. Jane held her up. Akiko felt as frail as a bird in her arms. She seemed to weigh nothing.

"Thank you," Akiko said. "It is the effort. The huge strain of bringing so many of the dead back to life. Telling them what to do. I do not know how much longer I can keep it up."

"You have to," Jane said. "You don't have a choice. Tom and Mai are counting on you. You can't give up, Akiko-san. Not now."

Chapter 14
Payback Time

Tom's head was starting to clear. He dragged himself to his feet and drew a pair of *sai* from his belt.

The Lord of Fire was still beating up Mai. His fists made horrible wet smacking sounds as they hit her.

Tom was about to charge at him with the *sai*.

Then he saw a human shape out of the corner of his eye.

A man in white.

A Shinobi Ghost.

Moving fast.

Tom grinned. *Good work, Akiko. In the nick of time.*

More Shinobi Ghosts followed behind the first one. They darted across the arena, crowding round the Lord of Fire.

Their feet didn't make a sound. The Lord of Fire had his back to them. He wouldn't have known they were coming if the demons hadn't told him. They shouted out a warning.

The Lord of Fire turned round just as the first of the Shinobi Ghosts attacked. At once the Lord of Fire dropped Mai in order to defend himself. Mai slumped to the floor. Her face was swollen and bloody.

The Shinobi Ghost had a *naginata*. He slashed it down at the Lord of Fire from above. The Lord of Fire blocked the blow with his forearm, stopping the *naginata's* blade from hitting his head. At the same time he punched the Shinobi Ghost in the chest. His fist went straight through, coming out of the Shinobi Ghost's back. The Shinobi Ghost collapsed.

Another of the Shinobi Ghosts ran at the Lord of Fire, whirling a *nunchaku*. The Lord of Fire breathed a huge burst of fire. The Shinobi Ghost went up in flames. He reeled, his clothing ablaze. He fell, just a heap of charred, smoking bones.

The remaining Shinobi Ghosts formed a circle round the Lord of Fire, several deep. The Lord of Fire twisted his head to and fro, looking at them all. He let out a scornful laugh.

Then he turned to Tom. "So you've asked your great-aunt for help too, eh? Was it hard, having to swallow your pride and go crawling to her? I think it must have been. Still, you were desperate. And that's what this smacks of."

He pointed at the Shinobi Ghosts.

"Desperation. Do you really think these puppets are going to stop me? *Me?* It won't take me a minute to polish them off."

"Go ahead, then," said Tom. "See how fast you can do it, Dragon."

"Stop calling me that," said the Lord of Fire. "It's not my name. There's no such person as Dragon. There never was. Dragon was nothing but a mask I wore for a while."

"Whatever. Just get on with it. Show us all your mighty powers. Show us how nothing can stop you now."

"Very well, I will."

A Shinobi Ghost leapt forward, waving a *tanto* dagger in the air. The Lord of Fire bent down under the dagger strike. He *karate-*chopped the Shinobi Ghost's arm, snapping it at the elbow. The Shinobi Ghost threw a palm-heel punch with his other arm. The Lord of

Fire broke that arm too. Then, with a roundhouse kick, he knocked the Shinobi Ghost's head clean off.

As the headless Shinobi Ghost toppled over, another of them stepped up to tackle the Lord of Fire.

One by one the Shinobi Ghosts attacked. One by one the Lord of Fire finished them off. It was amazing how fast he did it. Soon there were none left. The arena floor was littered with their bodies.

The Lord of Fire looked down on the fallen Shinobi Ghosts with a scornful grin. He put his hand up and felt the necklace with the Element Gems.

"There," he said. "That wasn't really a challenge. Now, where has that stupid boy got to?"

"I'm here," said Tom.

Tom had sneaked up on the Lord of Fire while he'd been busy fighting the Shinobi Ghosts. Now he was standing right behind him.

"The Shinobi Ghosts weren't meant to be a challenge, Dragon," Tom said. "They were there just to distract you for a moment or two."

And he lashed out with two *sai*.

The Lord of Fire moved aside with amazing speed. The tip of one of the *sai* blades brushed his neck. The other made no contact with his body at all. It simply shot past his waist.

"Missed," he said. "So slow, Tom. And your mind is so easy to read. I knew you'd use your two *sai* just like that. I always know what you're going to do, almost before *you* know. And that's why you can't win."

"Oh, yeah?" said Tom. "So you'll know what I'm going to do next, and just teleport yourself out of the way, right?"

"If I wish to."

"Then here it comes. *Hai!*" Tom stabbed at the Lord of Fire with just one of his *sai*.

The Lord of Fire didn't move. He just stood there with a puzzled look on his face.

"I didn't teleport," he said.

He looked down. The *sai* was sticking out of his belly.

"No, you didn't," Tom said. "Want to know why?"

He held up the other *sai*. The string of Element Gems was hanging from it, hooked over the centre blade, its loose ends dangling down.

"Because I've got this," Tom said. "I cut it off and snatched it from you in that first attack."

"Give me that!" the Lord of Fire yelled. He made a grab for the necklace.

Tom stepped to one side.

The Lord of Fire fell to the ground, his fists clutching nothing but empty air.

Tom turned towards the thrones.

"Guys?" he said to the other four Lords of Pain. He waved his *sai*. "Look here. Your Element Gems. The ones the Lord of Fire stole. Want them back?"

The four Lords of Pain all rose to their feet.

"Give them to us," the Lord of Tears demanded. "Now!"

"In a moment," Tom said. "Before I do, I want you to remember something." He pointed to the Lord of Fire, who was twisting and turning on the floor, trying to pull the *sai* out from his belly. "I want you to remember how he betrayed you. Double-crossed you. Used the power of your gems."

The four Lords of Pain closed in on Tom and the Lord of Fire. Their eyes blazed with rage. The crowd of demons had fallen silent.

"He was one of you," Tom went on. "Your friend. Your ally. But what was it he called you just now? 'Fools', wasn't it? And he said he wished he'd stolen your powers ages ago. Some friend!"

The Lord of the Mountain ground his teeth, loud as an earth-quake. The Lord of the Typhoon flapped his wings, loud as thunder.

"Now's your chance to show him how you feel about that," Tom said. "He's down. He's yours to do with as you please. Payback time, I'd say."

"Yes," hissed the Lord of the Void. "Oh, yes!"

"Just thought I'd point that out. Here you go then." Tom plucked the necklace off the *sai* and tossed it at the four Lords of Pain. "Catch!"

The Lord of the Typhoon got there first. He snatched the necklace out of the air. He tugged the green Element Gem off it with a cry of triumph.

Then the Lord of the Mountain grabbed the necklace from him. He took off the grey Element Gem.

The Lord of Tears was next. Then the Lord of the Void.

At last, all of them had their Element Gems back, safe in their grasp. They hugged them to their chests. The Gems sank through their flesh, into their hearts. The four Lords of Pain looked strong again. Grinning with glee, they turned on the Lord of Fire.

"No!" the Lord of Fire gasped. The other Lords of Pain were closing in on him. He pleaded with them. "Don't! I didn't mean what I said. I was just showing off. You aren't fools. You're fine, fine arch-demons. I'm proud to call you my equals. I took your gems just because I wanted us to win for once. That was all. After all this time, all those defeats, I just wanted to win!"

The other four were on every side of him.

"No!" he begged them. "I'm a Lord of Pain. Like you."

They bent down.

"We're all Lords of Pain. We're all the same."

"Yes," said the Lord of the Mountain. "Lords of *Pain*."

119

Tom turned away.

The Lord of Fire began to scream. And there were sounds of tearing, and cracking, and crunching, and squishing. Awful sounds.

The Lord of Fire's screams went on and on for a very long time.

Tom blocked them out as best he could. He went over to Mai. She was only just alive. He picked her up and began carrying her towards the doors. He could hear the crowd of demons whimpering in horror. He didn't look back. He got to the doorway. He still didn't look back. The Lord of Fire's screams turned to choking gasps, then to silence.

Tom stepped out through the shimmering curtain into the cold night air. His mother said his name. Relief was written all over her face. It shivered in her voice.

Tom laid Mai down on the ground. Great-aunt Akiko knelt down beside her granddaughter. She let out a howl of distress.

The doors of Canterbury Cathedral slammed shut behind Tom. They slammed shut so hard, it seemed they might never open again.

Chapter 15
Holiday in the Sun

Hot sun shone down. Palm trees cast dappled shadows on the sand. Waves tumbled gently against the beach, blue water turning to creamy white. Somewhere in the distance a steel band was playing the Bob Marley song "Three Little Birds". The sound rippled and swayed. It was music that said *Everything's OK. Every little thing is going to be all right.*

Tom's mother came out of the sea. She shook shiny drops of water from her hair.

"It's fantastic," she said, walking up to the top of the beach, where Tom lay on a sun-bed. "You should have a dip."

"I will," said Tom. He snuggled down on the sun bed. "Later. I'm pretty happy here right now."

"Fine," said his mother. "I'm going back up to the hotel to dry off and get changed. It's nearly lunch. Sword-fish steaks and sweet potatoes. Forget my diet, I'm going to stuff my face!"

She went off.

Tom turned to the sun-bed next to his. "All right, Sharif?"

"Never better, mate." Sharif had been lying in the sun every day for the past week, getting himself an all-over tan. Now he was as brown as a nut, and his scars hardly showed any more.

Tom's own scars would soon be gone. He'd booked in to see the consultant, the plastic surgeon Dr Franks, next month.

Just about then, Tom and his mother would also be moving back into their flat. The painters had promised that all the rooms would be done by then. Tom had seen plans of how the place would look. It was going to be one cool-looking flat.

"This holiday was a brill idea," Sharif went on. "Your mum's a star. And I'll tell you something else. She looks pretty hot in a swimsuit."

"Sharif," said Tom, "I'm going to try to forget you ever said that."

"I'm just saying she's fit, that's all. For an old bird."

"You've gone way beyond creepy, Sharif. Stop it right now."

Sharif just laughed.

Tom's mobile bleeped. He saw he had one new text message and one new voice-mail message.

The text was from Debbie.

Hope ur havng a gr8 time u jammy dodger. Think of us back in rainy old England. Can't wait to c u when u get back. x Deb

Tom grinned and thumbed her a quick reply.

Missng u. Sun sea & sand nothing compared 2 ur smile. x Tom

A bit corny, he thought, but Debbie wouldn't mind. He could just see her laughing as she read it. It gave him a warm, fuzzy feeling inside, knowing he could make Debbie Williams laugh.

The voice-mail was from Mai.

"Hey, True Warrior," she said. "Chop-socky Chick here. Checking in. Giving you an update on how I'm doing, like you asked me to. I'm doing OK, actually. My face doesn't look like an elephant stomped on it any more. The bruises are amazing shades of brown and purple, but I'm looking more like me again. Dr Goto is very pleased with my progress. He said I'll soon be back to my usual gorgeous self. No lasting damage. He didn't quite say 'gorgeous'. But I'm sure he was thinking it. I've told you how cute Dr Goto is, haven't I? If I were ten years older ...

"Anyway, I just thought I should say well done, again. You did it, Tom. You won your Contest. I know I helped a bit, and my grandmother too, but it was you who did most of the work. That was a hell of a plan. I know you made some of it up as you went along, but even so. You're a star.

"And speaking of my grandmother, she wants me to tell you she's proud of you. She says you're a Yamada to the core, but you're also your own man. You did things your way, and it worked. And she says any time you want to come and visit us in Japan, you'd be welcome to. Your mother as well. Really. She really said that. 'He can bring his mother too.' I think those two have started to like each other. Stopped hating each other so much, at any rate.

"Oh, and Akiko says something else. She says she believes the Contest is over. Not just your Contest – we know that. She means the whole thing. After thousands of years. Finally over. She's looked at her tarot cards and talked with the spirits of her ancestors. They've been telling her that the Contest can't go on any more because there aren't *five* Lords of Pain any more. The Lord of Fire is dead.

The other four Lords of Pain utterly destroyed him. So now the terms of the Contest no longer apply, and therefore the Contest itself is null and void.

"That doesn't mean the demons won't ever try and take over the world again. But they'll have to come up with some other way of doing it. A Yamada won't have to face the Lords of Pain every 30 years. That's all over and done with. Our family is off the hook!

"So there. That's all the news for now from here in Japan. Enjoy your time in Bermuda. If anyone's earned a rest, Tom, it's you. *Sayonara!*"

Tom closed the phone.

"That was a long message," said Sharif.

"Yeah, it was."

"Good news?"

"Good. Really good."

"Going to tell me about it?"

Should I tell him? thought Tom. *I can now, can't I?*

"No, mate," he said at last. He picked up a glass of fresh mango juice from the table. He sipped it. The juice tasted cool and sunny and sweet. "It's just good news. Take it from me. The best. There's nothing to worry about."

He stretched out and gave a sigh.

The notes of "Three Little Birds" were still floating softly over to him, like music from a dream.

"Nothing to worry about at all."

List of Japanese Words

Akiko: female name; it means either "autumn child" or "bright child"

Baka: an insult in Japanese

Banzai: Japanese word sometimes used as a battle cry; it means "long life" or "hurrah!"

Chigiriki: type of club with a spiked, cylinder shaped weight attached to a chain at one end

Domo arigato: Japanese for "thank you"

Gaijin: Japanese word for an "outsider", anyone who isn't Japanese

Gi (say it with a hard g, like in 'go'): martial arts uniform. Loose trousers and a jacket tied at the waist with a cloth belt

Kama: a sickle (see picture)

Kanji: Japanese writing

Katana: long sword used by warriors, such as the samurai (see picture)

Kata: pattern of movements used for learning and practising martial arts

Konnichiwa: "good afternoon", "good evening" in Japanese

Mai: female name; it means "dance"

Naginata: pole weapon ending in a long, curved blade

Nunchaku: two short pieces of wood joined by a chain

Sai (sigh): dagger with prongs on either side (see picture)

Sayonara: Japanese for "goodbye"

Sensei (sen-say): polite name for a master or teacher

Shinobi: another word for ninja

Shuriken: a throwing-star made of iron (see picture)

Tanto: 30-centimetre-long dagger

Tomeo: Tom's full name; in Japanese it means "man who takes no risks"

FIVE DEMONS.
ONE WARRIOR.
NO SECOND CHANCES.

WANT TO FIND OUT
MORE ABOUT
THE 5 LORDS
OF PAIN?

CHECK OUT
THE WEBSITE!

WWW.FIVELORDSOFPAIN.CO.UK

Barrington Stoke would like to thank all its readers for commenting on the manuscript before publication and in particular:

Lizzie Alder
Richard Brant
Polly Byrne
Joshua Caddy
Andrew Campbell
Mary Campbell
Sean Campbell
John Cowe
Ryan Crowle
Billy Elliott
Brandon Ellis
George Evans
Ronnie Forsythe
Jake Francis

Robert Garside
Sue Gillespie
CJ Lethbridge
Chris McClury
Nathan Morgan
Thomas Pearman
Tré Pusey
Sam Quarterman
Martisha Thompson
Jordan Truscott
Rachael Sargent
Haydn Smallwood
Kim Wherry
James Wright

Become a Consultant!

Would you like to be a consultant? Ask your parent, carer or teacher to contact us at the email address below – we'd love to hear from them! They can also find out more by visiting our website.

schools@barringtonstoke.co.uk
www.barringtonstoke.co.uk